E   389276
Hay   13.69
Hayes
This is the bear

This Is the Bear
First published in England by Walker Books Ltd, London.
Text copyright © 1986 by Sarah Hayes
Illustrations copyright © 1986 by Helen Craig
Printed in Italy. All rights reserved.
Library of Congress Catalog Card No. 85-45752
ISBN 0-397-32171-6
1 2 3 4 5 6 7 8 9 10
First American Edition

THIS IS THE
BEAR

by Sarah Hayes

illustrated by Helen Craig

J. B. Lippincott   New York

This is the bear

who fell in the bin.

This is the dog
who pushed him in.

This is the man
who picked up the sack.

This is the driver

who would not come back.

This is the bear
who went to the dump

and fell on the pile
with a bit of a bump.

This is the boy

who took the bus

and went to the dump
to make a fuss.

This is the man
in an awful grump

who searched
and searched
and searched the dump.

This is the bear
all cold and cross

who never thought

he was really lost.

This is the dog
who smelled the smell

of a bone

and a can

and a bear as well.

This is the man
who drove them home –

the boy, the bear
and the dog with a bone.

This is the bear
neat as a pin

who would not say

just where he had been.

This is the boy

who knew quite well,

but promised his friend

he would not tell.

And this is the boy
who woke up in the night
and asked the bear
if he felt all right –
and was very surprised
when the bear gave a shout,
"How soon can we have
another day out?"